KT-528-939

OUCH!!!

Poor Puppy, his foot hurts!

Mummy kisses Puppy.
Then she rubs his foot and says...

279889

F

Let me kiss *it* better

Illustrated by

Mamoru Hiraide

FALKIRK COUNCIL
LIBRARY SUPPORT
FOR SCHOOLS

Oops!

Pain, pain, go away...

"Mummy, where did the pain go?"
asks Puppy.

Mummy thinks for a moment.
"I don't know..." she says.

Little Puppy runs outside.

"I am going to look for it,"
he says.

Now, where could the pain have gone?

Scrape

Scrape

Scrape

Puppy sees a lump on the ground.

Is this where it's gone?

NO!!!

It's only Mr Mole!

But, where could the pain have gone?

Hey, are the clouds crying?

Is this where it's gone?

NO! It's only Mr. Cloud!

Puppy looked under the rainbow...

In the bushes...

...in the water

OUCH!!!
Now Puppy has found it again!

Pain, pain, go away...

Friendly Fox leans over
to rub Puppy's head.

Pain, pain, go away...

This really works!
So Puppy does the same
for Friendly Fox.

Once again, the pain has gone!

The two of them look at each other
and giggle.

"So, did you find the pain, love?" asks Mummy.

"Yes, I did...
but we made it go away again.
And, I've found something else..."

"...a new friend!"